W9-ART-190

Copyright © 1994 by Milton Bradley Company, a division of Hasbro, Inc.
All rights reserved under International and Pan-American Copyright Conventions. Published in the United States by Random House, Inc., New York. CANDY LAND is a trademark of Hasbro, Inc.

Library of Congress Cataloging-in-Publication Data
Alvarez, Cynthia.
The Candy Land mystery / by Cynthia Alvarez.
    p. cm.
SUMMARY: When the wicked Lord Licorice casts a spell that makes King Kandy's castle disappear, the Candy Land Kids must use their noses to find the cinnamon scent that will lead them to the king.
ISBN 0-679-86200-5
1. Scented books—Specimens. [1. Candy—Fiction. 2. Magic—Fiction. 3. Scented books. 4. Toy and movable books.] I. Title.
PZ7.A479Can 1994 [E]—dc20 93-42828

Manufactured in the United States of America   10 9 8 7 6 5 4 3 2 1

THE CANDY LAND™ MYSTERY

by Cynthia Alvarez

illustrated by Bobbi Barto

Random House New York

The Candy Land Kids could not believe their eyes. Candy Castle had disappeared! In its place was a sign from the wicked Lord Licorice.

King Kandy, the Imperial Head Bonbon and Grand Jujube of Candy Land, was missing!

"We have to find him," said the Candy Land Kids.

"The King's castle has such a wonderful cinnamon smell," they continued. "If we follow our noses, I bet we can track down the King and his castle!"

So with their noses sniffing and whiffing, the Candy Land Kids started their search.

Citizens of Candy Land:

I have cast a spell on King Kandy. No one will ever find him or his castle. Candy Land is now mine!

Your New King,
Lord Licorice

Their first stop was Plumpy's. Plumpy was the last of the PlumpaTrolls and the caretaker of the Gingerbread Plum Trees.

"King Kandy is missing? So that's why my plums aren't perfectly plump! But the Gingerbread Plum Trees still smell delicious. Take a sniff."

The Candy Land Kids smelled the bark of the plum trees. The trees smelled like fresh-baked gingerbread, but there wasn't a trace of cinnamon anywhere.

Next they came upon Mr. Mint. He was busy carving a flute out of a peppermint tree.

"What? The King is missing?" he cried. "No wonder my peppermint piccolos sound off-key! Lord Licorice will make mincemeat of my music if he becomes king!"

Was the King hidden in the forest? The Candy Land Kids sniffed and sniffed. But the Peppermint Forest just smelled like mint. With hearts pounding, they continued on their way to the next stop—the castle of Lord Licorice!

When they got there, who should be waiting for them but...Lord Licorice himself, the wickedest man ever.

"You will never find King Kandy," sneered Lord Licorice. His heart was as hard as rock candy.

How could someone so sour be named for such a sweet-smelling candy? the Candy Land Kids wondered. "Let's get out of here and head for Gumdrop Mountains!"

When they reached the colorful hills, Jolly, the Official Gumdrop Mountain Greeter, said, "I knew something strange was happening! My Gumdrop Mountains are all mixed up. The orange mountains smell like lemons! Smell for yourself. Take a whiff."

Jolly was right. All of the mountains were mixed up—
but none of them smelled cinnamony, like Candy Castle.
The Candy Land Kids decided to visit Gramma Nutt next.

Something was not right at Gramma Nutt's. Her Peanut Brittle House was usually in tiptop shape. But today, pieces of brittle were breaking off the roof, and peanuts were popping off the walls!

Poor Gramma Nutt was in such a tizzy she could scarcely speak.

"Don't worry about me," said Gramma Nutt. "You run along and find King Kandy."

So the Candy Land Kids did just that, making tracks for Lollipop Woods.

Queen Frostine was doing her best to comfort Princess Lolly, King Kandy's daughter.

"My lollipop trees stopped growing—even the baby cherry trees!" cried Princess Lolly. "I miss my daddy, the King."

The Candy Land Kids were feeling glummer than a stick that had lost its lolly. Were they never going to find the King? They sniffed Princess Lolly's cherry trees. Alas, they smelled like cherries, not cinnamon. But Queen Frostine would not let them give up.

"You will *find* King Kandy and *save* Candy Land!" she said. "I'm sure of it."

But how? the Candy Land Kids wondered. Then they remembered the one place they hadn't looked—Molasses Swamp!

Gloppy, the gooey Molasses Monster, was taking
a nap on a very big, lumpy pillow in Molasses Swamp.
Gloppy yawned and scratched his gooey tummy.

"Look at this enormous pillow I found!" he said sleepily. "It's a little lumpy and it smells funny, but I like it."

The Candy Land Kids sniffed. It smelled funny, all right. It smelled just like...*cinnamon!*

"It's King Kandy and the Candy Castle!" the Candy Land Kids shouted.

They pulled Gloppy's giant pillow out of the swamp and rinsed it off with lemonade. King Kandy appeared underneath, and in a twinkle, the Candy Castle appeared on the edge of Molasses Swamp. Both the King and his castle were safe and sound.

"Hooray!" shouted the Candy Land Kids as they hugged the King. "Lord Licorice's spell is broken!"

"Thank you for saving me!" said King Kandy. "But how did you ever find me?"

The Candy Land Kids traded secret smiles and said, "We just followed our noses!"

As the King and the Candy Land Kids strolled back down the lanes of Candy Land, they watched as, one by one, all traces of Lord Licorice's wicked spell disappeared. Princess Lolly's lollipop trees grew straight and tall. Gramma Nutt's house pulled itself together. Jolly's orange mountains stopped smelling like lemons. Mr. Mint's piccolos piped sweetly. And Plumpy's plums grew perfectly plump.

Thanks to the Candy Land Kids, Candy Land was a sweet place once again!